MILLY'S WEDDING

Kate Summers

ILLUSTRATED BY

Maggie Kneen

Orion
Children's Books

Milly Town Mouse was getting married. By chance she had met Tom Brown Mouse down by the canal, one moonlit night.

Tom was on a bank, nibbling cheese.
Milly was by the bridge.
They looked. They blinked.

And fell in love.

In the days that followed, Tom and Milly often went walking along the tow path. Milly loved the brightly painted boats moored by the bank.

One day Tom showed Milly where he lived. It was a narrowboat, beautifully decorated, with flowers growing on the deck.

"Come aboard," said Tom.
The boat was rocking gently. Milly could hear
the water *lap-lap-lapping* against the side.
"I wish it would keep still!" she said.

So Tom took Milly by the paw and helped her
on to the boat.

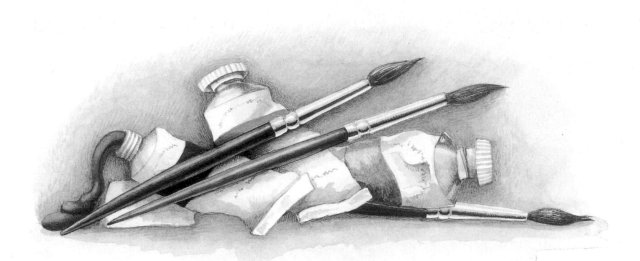

Milly followed Tom down a ladder, to a room below the deck. It was full of pictures, paper and paint, all in a muddle.
"Goodness!" said Milly with a sigh.

Tom pointed to a portrait on the wall. "That's me," he said. "You have very fine whiskers," said Milly.

Then the two mice clambered inside a cupboard,
where Tom had made himself a home.

"I know it's not much of a place *now*," he said.
"But with some wallpaper, tables, chairs . . .
ANYTHING you wish – I could make the best
house for . . . us. Oh, Milly! Will you marry me?"

"Yes," said Milly. "I will!"

So, Tom and Milly were
engaged to be married.
Tom gave Milly a heart-shaped
twist of lavender to wear.

Milly took Tom to meet her parents.
Mr and Mrs Town Mouse thought Tom would
make a very good husband for their daughter.

Then they all got busy with plans for the wedding.
There was so much to do, and not very much time
before the wedding day.

Tom and Milly sent invitations to their families
and friends. There were lots of them! They had
brothers and sisters all over town.

And, of course,
Milly wanted her friend
Tilly, who lived in the
country, to come.
"I must go and see her at once," she told Tom.
"I have something important to ask her."

Early next morning Milly set off for the country. It was a long walk but, at last, she found the little lane that led to Tilly's house.

Tilly was very excited to see her friend again, and squeaked when she heard Milly's news.
"Will you be my Chief Bridesmaid?" asked Milly.
"Of course!" said Tilly. "I'll make your wedding dress too."

After a lunch of freshly baked
bread and hazelnut spread,
they looked at dress patterns.
They chose ones that were just
right for Milly and her bridesmaids.

"How many bridesmaids will there be?" asked Tilly.
"Six," said Milly. "There's Berry, Pip, Clover and
April . . . and the twins, Hoppy and Skip."

Tilly measured Milly carefully. Then she cut out the
pattern in paper, and pinned the pieces together.
"Tomorrow," she said, "we shall buy the very best
silk for your dress."

Next day Tilly took Milly to a big mulberry tree.
It was full of silkworms eating leaves.

Tilly told her that they could make silk.
"Each silkworm spins a cocoon from fine sticky
threads," she explained. "Each tiny thread
becomes a strand of glossy silk."

At the foot of the tree they
found Mrs Weaver Mouse.
She was winding the silk
strands on to reels,
ready for weaving.

And piled high were
rolls of silk in the
prettiest colours –
apple blossom, peach,
apricot, corn . . .
every colour you
could imagine.

"I should like tea-rose pink
for my dress,
and forget-me-not blue for
the bridesmaids,"
said Milly.

Meanwhile Tom had been busy on the boat.
He was a handy mouse, clever with his paws at
woodwork and plumbing.

Some friends came to help too.
Together they planned to turn the cupboard into
a splendid home in no time!

They found everything they needed lying on the floor. Soon there was the sound of many mice

hammering,

sawing,

scrubbing,

scraping,

plastering

and papering   all at once.

One afternoon Tom was fixing a shower in the bathroom. But when he turned on the taps, the shower spun round and round.

By the time Tom could turn the taps off again, he was in a puddle right up to his knees.

At that moment Tom's uncle, a seafaring mouse called Captain Longtail, came to visit. "Ahoy, there! Tom," he said. "You look as wet as a fish!"

While Tom was mopping
up the mess, he told his
uncle all about Milly.

When Milly arrived back
from the country,
Tom introduced her to his uncle.

"I'll marry the pair of you myself," said Captain
Longtail. "I've married lots of mice at sea,
but yours will be the grandest wedding of
the year!"

At last it was Milly's wedding day.
Tilly arrived early at Milly's house, with six excited
little bridesmaids. They were each carrying a box
with their dresses neatly packed inside.

Tilly opened the biggest box and showed Milly
her dress. Milly gasped. "It's *beautiful*," she said.
"Oh, Tilly! You are the cleverest
mouse in the world!"

Tilly laughed.
"Let me help you
put it on," she said.
"I only hope
it fits!"

Milly's dress was like a summer rose in full bloom.
Tilly had embroidered the bodice with hearts and
flowers, and had stitched a tiny silver acorn there,
just for luck.

Milly twirled round
and round in front
of the mirror.
She looked lovely
and the dress
fitted perfectly.

"Can I put my dress on now?"
squealed the smallest
bridesmaid called Pip.
"Of course," said Tilly.
"It's time we all got ready."

Back at the boat Tom was
putting on his new suit.
His brother, Sam, who was
Best Mouse, was there too.

"Have you got the ring?" asked Tom anxiously.
"Yes," said Sam.
"Where?" said Tom.
"In my pocket," said Sam.
"Which one?" said Tom.
"This one," said Sam,
patting his waistcoat.
"It will be quite safe, don't worry."

Then Tom tried on his top hat.
But, oh dear! It was much too big.
"The shop has sent the wrong
size!" he said.

Sam looked at his watch. There wasn't much time. The wedding was in less than an hour! He would have to hurry.

So he ran as fast as he could to the shop to fetch a smaller hat. On the way back, he took a short cut across the canal, skipping from barge to barge.

He took a flying leap on to the towpath,

tripped over a coil of rope and . . .

SPLASH! The ring fell into the water!

Sam could see the ring glinting in the sun.
There was nothing for it. He would have to use
Tom's top hat for a boat, and fish it out.

Sam launched the hat and pushed off with a twig.
By now the ring was sinking fast!

Sam leaned over the brim,
hooked the ring with his
twig and clutched it in
his paw.

"Phew!" he sighed. "To think I nearly lost it."

When Sam got back to the boat, he found Tom
pacing up and down, looking worried.
"You've been a long time," he said.
"I'm sorry," said Sam. "I stopped to . . . er . . .
do a spot of fishing."

"So I see," said Tom. "My hat is dripping wet!"

Up on deck, Captain Longtail had ordered his crew to form a Guard of Honour. The mouse sailors looked very smart in their uniforms, as they stood stiffly to attention.

Then, as the first guests arrived, a band of musicians began to play some tunes.

Soon the deck was crowded with happy chattering mice, all wearing their best coats and gowns.

Milly's mother was dressed in green, with satin shoes to match. Her grandmother wore velvet, and a bonnet trimmed with lace.

You never saw so many mice together all at once!

At exactly twelve o'clock,
Milly and her bridesmaids
arrived.

Milly and her father sat in a carriage pulled by
two shiny stag beetles. Tilly and the young
bridesmaids came in a wagon.

Mr Town Mouse helped his
daughter down from the carriage.
And when everyone was ready,
they walked up the
gangplank.

Tom was waiting for Milly on deck. He thought
she was the most beautiful mouse he had ever
seen. Milly smiled as she held his paw.

The wedding had begun.

Captain Longtail read the marriage service from a book while Tom and Milly listened carefully. They promised to love and care for each other always.

Then Sam passed the ring to Tom,
and Tom gave it to Milly.
"You may kiss the bride," said the captain.

And so Tom and Milly were married.

Afterwards Mr and Mrs Brown Mouse had their photographs taken. It took quite a time.

First there were pictures
of the bride and groom,
Tom and Milly.

Then there were pictures
of the bridesmaids . . .

and Tom with Sam . . .
and Milly with Tilly . . .

and, last of all,
Tom and Milly with . . .

EVERYONE!

"Now let's eat," said Tom. "I'm hungry!"
Then he and Milly led the way to an enormous
table, spread with wonderful food.

When everyone had eaten and drunk as much as
they were able, Sam gave a speech. He tried to tell
them about the ring, and how he had used Tom's
hat as a boat.

Everyone laughed until
tears rolled down their
cheeks. But no one,
except Tom, believed him.

Then Tom and Milly cut their wedding cake.

It was tier upon tier
of the richest,
creamiest
cheesecake
imaginable.
Each slice
a delicious
mouth-
watering
delight.

Later that evening
when they were alone
Milly whispered,
"I love you,
Tom Brown Mouse."
"I love you too,"
said Tom.

And they danced in the glow
of the pale harvest moon.